THE
SECRET
OF
DREAMS

PARALYSIS

DISVON RAYFORD

Ordering Information:

Prime Seven Media
518 Landmann St.
Tomah City, WI 54660

Printed in the United States of America

TABLE OF CONTENTS

CHAPTER 1

THE MEANING OF DREAMS

LORI: Dreams are strange, aren't they? You never really know what they mean, if they even have a meaning at all. You try to decipher them, and even sometimes see a shrink, hoping they can just give you the straight answers. But of course, that isn't how dreams work. They torment us. Sometimes, they're good and you don't want to wake up from them. Other times, they're bad, and you want nothing more than to wake up. But dreams can sometimes seem real, and those dreams sometimes are referred to as deja vu. If you know anything at all about sleep paralysis, then you know they are referred to as waking nightmares. These are often experienced by coma patients. But even more intriguing about coma patients is that they sometimes wake up and seem to have different personalities. This has never been explained properly. Some say it's just the effect of being asleep for so long. But I found it fascinating that nobody really looked into why they would suffer memory loss. Like, they would remember certain parts of their lives but not anything else. What was this about? Why was it such a common thing amongst coma patients? Or, even those who have suffered spiritual attacks, such as possession. What was this phenomenon?

I had to know. After all, I didn't get this Bachelor's in Journalism for nothing. Lori Segrin. A very well known journalist. Taking the hard risks, asking the tough questions, facing down the city's most corrupt and filthy rich. That's me. But sometimes I felt like that person was somebody else. What did I really want in life? To find a husband. Settle down. Have children. But I'm thirty-five years old, and highly doubt my chances. I was smoking a cigarette outside of Osterling, Maine's only hospital. I had some questions for a certain C.E.O, but I knew I'd get snubbed, but still had to try. It was raining and I was just standing outside of the main entrance. I was watching doctors and nurses walk out for lunch. It was afternoon, and I couldn't help but think about the current rumors. Next Level Advancements. A company that prided itself on creating things no other corporation had even thought of. They were the first to make a cell phone that comes with the ability to make a phone call, no matter where you are. Everyone knew that they made a satellite whose signal was so strong that it sometimes blocked out other signals and overpowered everything else. The signal jammed other satellite's signals and now we have to rely solely on NLA's. They took over the satellite business. Even the ones placed up there by Uncle Sam. I saw my prey approaching. She had just come out of a coma. It was a strange and sudden coma that nobody seemed to be able to explain. She was too young to just have a heart attack, but that is what happened, apparently. "Hi, Ms...", "Move.", she said. Shoving me. I was pissed, but I couldn't get to her now. Her security was waiting not too far away. I put out my cigarette, and made my way home.

As I walked in, I went into my investigation room, as I liked to call it, and sat down with my research. As most corporations often have, there was a shady past to NLA, and they were involved in shady things under the table. I was investigating one thing, though, in particular that supposedly could be catastrophic for the whole planet. You hear environmentalists harp on and on about how we're killing the planet. But I heard from my contacts, NLA can do it with one single blow. All it takes is the wrong point to be moved about, and then the whole planet could be moved off it's axis, and we would be fucked. No way to fix it. Now the planet does this often anyway, but it would be a catastrophe if NLA proceeds with their plan Maybe NLA had a back-up plan. I didn't know. But they wanted to drill into the Earth to access the core for resources. It is literally the most selfish thing you can imagine. It could kill everyone. If this was true, of course. I was told they were denied by the Supreme Court, so that's ONE saving grace, despite the fact the court is filled with crazy old farts. As I was doing some research on what reaching the core could really do, my phone rang, "Segrin...", I said. "It's done. It's all over, Lori. We weren't able to stop them... We're dead...", said Tommy. He was my contact who knew what NLA was up to. "I'm sure there is someone who can...", I began to say. "Lori, you're not hearing me. They drilled, what Nasa said would happen, HAS happened, and now, they are scrambling to see if it can be fixed. But my sources say that it's irreversible.", "So, what are you saying then, Tommy?", "I'm saying how would you like to spend your last days?", said Tommy, now hanging up the phone. I fell back into my seat. I was panicking. I didn't even know how long we had until the geographical effects started to take place. I was angry. I tried to speak with the C.E.O before, but now, I didn't care.

I hopped into my car, started the engine, still angry, and drove to where I know that bitch lives. She didn't have security there to protect her.

I saw her house coming up down the road. My cell phone rang, "What?", I said. "Lori, this is Mr. Canter. I know that you tried approaching the NLA C.E.O today. What the hell is wrong with you? I told you not to go anywhere near her. She's suing you.", said Canter, the company attorney. "Do you know what they've done?", I asked, trying to contain myself. "I'm sure it isn't worth this lawsuit.", "They've destroyed the planet.", I said, hanging up the phone. Considering that we were going to die, none of this mattered anymore. I busted through her gates, not caring about anything. I took my gun out of my glove compartment, and ran into her house. As I walked in, I couldn't believe what I was seeing. There was a man sitting in a chair. He was sort of thirty-ish looking, and he had a bullet in his skull. I lowered my weapon. "You're late.", said a female voice from the top of the staircase. I pointed my gun up at her. "Ms. Segrin…", she said, coming down the stairs, with a drink in her hand. "I can't believe you…", I said. "Are you going to shoot me? Or do you want to live?", she said. I didn't know what to think. "You caused the planet to move off its axis, and somehow you think we can survive that?", I asked, raising my gun towards her face. "Well, I happen to know that we can. That YOU have.", "What the hell are you talking about?", "Follow me.", she said, going back up the stairs. I followed her, but kept my gun at her back. She led me to what looked like a laboratory in her home. "Why did you kill your husband?", I asked. "He wasn't my husband. He belonged to someone else. But it doesn't matter. You matter. And I'm going to make sure you live. It won't be easy, Lori.", "Why would you want to save my life?", I asked. "Because, you'll owe me.", she said, as I was grabbed from behind. I tried to turn and shoot, but the person punched me and I was knocked out.

When I came to, I was inside some kind of pod. I was laying on my back. I couldn't see exactly where I was. I saw people moving around me, and I started banging on the lid. But everyone was ignoring me. I started crying, thinking that this is how I was going to die. Then, a voice spoke into my pod, "Ms. Segrin, you aren't alone. We are all getting into these pods. Someone paid good money for you to be here, so you better be damn glad.", said a male voice. I didn't understand what the hell was happening. A loud noise started to sound off, and I covered my ears. The next thing I knew, I was back in my apartment.

CHAPTER 2

NIGHTMARES AND CREATIONS

HUSAN: "This is madness...", I said, as I was reading over the reports again. The drill had made it to the core. We began extracting minerals successfully. But, we thought we had figured out how to do this without the taking of egress from the planet. Allowing us to actually do this without paying an ultimate price, as often most do in the pursuit of power. But I now realize, with this ability to dream travel, perhaps this was already known. Perhaps our C.E.O knew the price we'd all pay for this... I had to confront her. She had come out of her coma. There were already journalists circling around her, wanting to question all of the political nonsense she's been spewing. I went into her office, my reports in hand. "Husan, I'm well aware. I'm assuming you've sent the emails out to your most loyal and trustworthy team members...", she said, not even looking at me. She was terrifying... She always has been. "I think we made a huge mistake... But something tells me you already know this...", I said, looking at her in fear. "True, I knew this planet would die. That's the way of the universe, Husan. Planets, stars, asteroids, all these things die. It's just this planet's time.", "You mean your words...", I said, realizing she truly is a monster. "You've read ReportZ, I'm assuming…", she said. "I thought it was preposterous…", "I'm glad you thought so. Because now you have no choice but to believe it.", she said, now standing up, and walking around her desk, "There is someone I want you to set a pod for. Lori Segrin.", "The reporter? Why? We're taking her?", "Believe it or not, she is quite important. We need her where we're going. So, just set up her pod.", "Is she aware?", "She knows about the drill, but if you're asking if she knows what's in ReportZ, no, she does not. She isn't a Next Level Advancements VIP, but she is still needed.", "Why?", I had to ask. "Everyone has a role to play, Husan. Even her. But I can't tell you why. Not yet. You'll see why.", she said, putting her coat on, "She'll be at my house. I expect you to be there around nine-thirty.", she said, leaving me in confusion.

I did as she asked. I had placed Segrin in a pod. She was strong, and took the medication nicely. She was most likely waking up. I knew it was time to get into my own pod. I did, and I felt the weak feeling that comes with sleep. I was reeling, but this was the only option now.

LORI: "Time for school.", I heard my mom say. I got out the bed, feeling lost. I looked at my mom, and realized that something was wrong. My mother wasn't young anymore. And this wasn't a happy situation. My mother was baking cookies. This seemed familiar. I looked in a mirror. I felt eight, but looked thirty. Where was I? How was I in my childhood home? I didn't want to be here. But still, something felt different. "Lori, come have some cookies before school.", said my mother. Something was not right. I walked into the kitchen, and saw something that made me freak out at first, but then I started to calm down. It was my stepfather, with a knife in his eye. He was sitting down quietly, not saying anything, but still alive. I was confused even more. I looked at the cookies my mom put on the table, and they all had a caricature of me on each one. Still confused, I took a cookie, and then my stepfather grabbed my hand, "YOU STUPID LITTLE BITCH! DID I SAY YOU CAN HAVE ONE OF MY COOKIES…?!", he shouted, and his voice echoed all crazy. I tried to take my hand from him, but he was holding it tightly. Then, the scene in my kitchen changed. I felt like I was seventeen now. I was about to leave, "Where are you going?", my stepfather said, coming from behind me. I slapped him, and he punched me. I was crawling across the floor, then a hand pulled me up, "COME ON!", yelled a woman. I was terrified, and I snatched my hand from her, but soon found myself falling. I didn't even know where I was falling.

When I landed, I looked around. I knew this place. This was my college. I went to a public college where eventually I earned enough credits to transfer to a university. In truth, I remember why I left. To get away from my mother. She wasn't as protective when she was with my stepfather, but after he died, suddenly she wanted to talk to me everyday. Bragging about her smart daughter. But this place I was in seemed to make me relive certain memories. This one is sad. I saw my mother approaching me and my friends. I was dating a guy named Brad. Brad had never met my mother. He was a nice guy. It's messed up what I did to him. But this was even MORE messed up. "LORI!", my mom yelled, rushing to hug me. She wrapped me in her arms and sunk her face into my shoulder. "GET OFF!", I yelled, pushing her away. She looked shocked, "Lori, what's wrong? I made your favorite type of cookies for you.", she said, reaching into her bag, and pulling out a baggie that had peanut butter cookies contained inside. She handed me the bag, "Oh, wow.", I said, looking at Brad. "It's nice to meet you, Mrs. Segrin…", said Brad, holding his hand out. "It's Mrs. Brady, actually…", said my mother. "Still using his name?", I asked. "Lori…", "No, you're still using his name?!", I yelled at my mother. "Lori, he's dead. Why can't you just let him be dead?", "Because you can't. You're still using his name.", "Lori, I'm sick of this. Despite what you did, I'm still here. I'm still your mother.". I opened the bag of cookies and threw them at her. She started to cry, and I picked up the cookies and crumpled them into her auburn colored hair. "LORI!", yelled Brad, who quickly grabbed me as I spit on my mother, who turned and left. That was the last conversation I had with her before she tried to kill herself. Now she's brain dead. "Don't you wish you could change that?", asked the woman who had tried to help me earlier. "Who are you?", I asked. "What if I told you I'm a really good friend you don't remember?", asked the woman. "Who are you?", I asked again. "Someone who you'll get to know. Now, let's talk about where you are…", said the woman, as the sky started to unveil. I felt myself being sucked into the sky, the woman was next to me.

When I woke up next, I found myself in my bed. I looked around and sat up. None of this made sense. I got up and went into my kitchen. My apartment was small. Living room, kitchen right next to it, my TV was sitting on my entertainment stand. I went into my investigation room, and saw nothing. All my work was gone. I became upset, and went to my wall and slapped my palm against it. "WHERE THE FUCK DID IT ALL GO?!", I yelled. I was angry. "Lori?". I turned around, and Brad was standing in my doorway. "Brad? What are you doing here?", I asked, shocked. This didn't make any sense. "I thought we were going out for lunch?", asked Brad, looking confused. I didn't know what else to do, so I put on some pants and a jacket and left with Brad.

We were at a burger joint. I kept looking around, because nothing made sense. "Lori, you haven't touched your food.", said Brad, looking at me strangely. I cheated on Brad with one of my professors. I got mad at him one day and bragged about it. Brad left me. But now we are together again? Make this make sense. "Brad… What's going on?", I asked. He just looked at me like I didn't know up from down. "Eat your fries… They'll make you feel better.". I just started to slowly eat my fries. A bus pulled up and was dropping people off. We were sitting outside. That's when I saw the label on the bus; Next Level Advancements. I saw her on the poster. Smiling like she wasn't an evil cunt. "Your sister is everywhere we look.", said Brad, chuckling. "Sister…? I don't have a sister…", I said. Because I don't. Now Brad got up and sat next to me, "Lori, your sister…", he said again. I just gave him the same confused look. "Stephanie… Stephanie Brady… Your sister… The CEO of NLA?", I dropped my jaw… "She isn't…", I was about to say. Then I looked around and realized what was off about this area. There seemed to be a dark figure just standing in the background. Watching, waiting, biding its time. I didn't know why. "Brad, I'm not feeling well.", "Yeah, when you forget your own sister, it's obvious.", he said, smiling, but still giving me a worried look.

Brad got me home. I was looking around my apartment, and realized there was a lot missing. "Get some rest…", said Brad. He left out my door.

I just fell onto my couch and fell asleep. When I woke up, something was working its way up my leg and thigh. I quickly tried to move, but I was stuck. The thing was just a shadow. No face, no mouth, no eyes. It looked up at me; It had a female form. She started to reach for my face, but then my door burst open. Stephanie Brady was standing in my doorway. The shadow person was gone. "Brad said you're not feeling well. What the hell is the matter now?", "We're not real sisters…", I said, still feeling weird. Stephanie looked at me for a few seconds, then she started to laugh, "OKAY!", she said sarcastically, "And what about this?", she said, brandishing pictures in her insanely, expensive wallet. I saw pictures of me, my mom, her dead ex-husband, and Stephanie. "No…", I said. "WHAT THE FUCK IS WRONG WITH YOU?!", yelled Steph, finally getting fed up with me. But still, something felt off. "I'm sorry…", I said. Steph just stared at me, "Do you need to see another shrink?", she asked me. "No, I just need some rest…", "Do you want me to stay here with you?". Just a few hours ago, I was pointing a gun at this woman. What was happening? "No… I'll be fine. I just need to sleep. Probably.", I said.

CHAPTER 3

MEMORIES OF SOMEONE ELSE

LORI: I was sitting in the office of Melanie Meyers. A therapist who costs a lot of money. Stephanie paid. She really loves me and wants me to get better. But I didn't even know who I was. Three days ago, my journalist instincts kicked in and I started to investigate this person that I suddenly had become. "Lori, we were talking about when you were eight. Remember?", asked Meyers. I just nodded, "Yeah… I remember growing up in a nice big blue and white house. I remember the windows on the front…", "Okay, and where are you lost?", "The part where Stephanie is Jack Brady's daughter…", "Considering that he was the President of NLA, I don't see how you're confused. The only diagnosis I can come up with is split personality disorder.", "I'm a Schizo?", "I don't like that term, so let's not call it that, please?", said Meyers, giving me a stern look, "You said that you studied journalism in college, but it says here that you have a Master's in business. You work closely with your sister.", "Then why am I living in a shitty apartment?", "That was your choice, Lori. Tell me about your relationship with Jack. When did he come into your life?", "When I was two, my dad died, and my mom met Jack a few months later.", "So, he was like an actual father, then?", "Sure. The only one I ever knew.", I said. The truth was, my mother met Jack when I was seven. I just told her the story of what I've learned of this new Lori. New Lori is a completely different person from me. She's kind, never cheated on any of her boyfriends, and actually respected Jack Brady. The Jack I knew was a nice guy. Until I accused him of something he didn't do. Then he became mean Jack. I kept pushing, though. Until he lost it. Tried to kill me. I used the attention from the story to make my wish come true. I got a job at one of the best news stations anyone could hope for. But all of this made no sense. Because now I work for NLA. "Listen, I understand if you feel stressed. I understand there is a big project going on.", said Meyers, writing on her notepad. "Yeah. Building a base on the moon…", I said. Stephanie may claim to love me as her sister, but she is still evil. Really evil. And somehow, I was involved. My connection was still fuzzy. But I wasn't about to tell this shrink that I'm from another universe. She'd have me committed. I needed someone who could help me with this. She definitely could not. "Lori, I'd like to continue these sessions. Remember, everything we discuss is between us. In the meantime, you're free to go. Your time is up.", "Okay. Thanks, Doc.", "Just call me Mel.", she said, as I nodded and walked out.

KEITH: I was watching Lori Segrin. She walked out of Melanie Meyer's office, then proceeded up towards 6th Ave. I followed her. I knew she was one of the transfers from Earth 5. As I followed her, I felt an intense headache. I looked up, and there stood the shadow. Watching me, and waiting as always for my guard to be down. I haven't slept since I got here, and of course I knew I wasn't alone. Lori on Earth 5 was investigating the company. I needed to get her on my side. I saw her go into the building's parking lot and quickly shouted to her, "HEY!", I yelled, catching up to her, and slamming her car door, "You don't know…me…", I said, trying to catch my breath, "But I work for your sister, and you need to get me out of here. Now. Something is after me, and I believe you have one too…", "One what?", asked Lori, now fully turning her attention to me. "A shadow…", I said, looking to see if mine was still watching me, but it had disappeared for the time being. "You work for NLA? What's your job?", "Dreamscaper…", "What the fuck is that…?", "You should know, Lori. You said it's too dangerous. You warned us…", "I didn't do anything like that…", "We need to speak with Husan Martin. He can confirm. At least I think he can. He's new. Most of the other transfers have fallen in line with Stephanie. But where we came from, you were investigating her…", I said, now giving her a hard look. Suddenly, it got really dark. "What's wrong with you?", asked Lori, as I suddenly started to freak out. I reached into my pocket and gave Lori my book of notes and ran away. "HEY! COME BACK!", yelled Lori, but I couldn't see anything anymore. "KEITH…", said a long, drawling, low, deep voice. I turned, and the shadow was following me. It was moving fast. "NO! STAY AWAY!", I yelled, trying to run, but now my body felt like it was in water. The shadow reached out to me, and I felt my head splitting, then I passed out.

LORI: I was confused. I looked at the little notebook in my hands, then realized that this was a NLA notebook. I opened it, and there were just squiggles and graphs. I decided I needed to go home and look at this. And what did he mean I have a shadow? What did that mean? Am I Peter Pan? I had no idea. I started to drive home, when I was hit with a very vivid memory.

"LORI! STEPANIE! Come on, girls, we're going to be late. We won't be able to skate if we come late!", "We're coming!", yelled Stephanie, who just smiled at me, "Can you believe he's finally taking us?", she said, really excited. I couldn't remember where we were going. I walked out of the room, and as usual, my mother was baking peanut butter cookies. Some were already done. I reached for them, and my step dad grabbed my hand playfully, "Now, did I say you can have one of these yet?", he asked, smiling at me. "No…", I said. He pulled me into a hug, "Today is going to be great! Sorry it took so long.", he said, now kissing my head, and walking away. I was really lost because my step dad and I did not get along like this. "Hey, you better make sure your sister stays out of trouble today.", said my mom, giving me a very stern look. Then, as if I could feel it standing next to me, the shadow with no face was next to me. It started to reach out and I ran. I left out the front door, but found myself in my college professor's study. I turned from the scene before me. I was letting him penetrate me from behind. He was a handsome man, but after this, I lost Brad. Something I never truly forgave myself for. The shadow was here now. It was watching the scene, and I heard a strange murmur coming from where the mouth was supposed to be. It looked at me, then started to walk towards me again. I just fell and cowered, "WHAT DO YOU WANT!?", I yelled.

"YOU STUPID BITCH! PAY ATTENTION!", a driver yelled at me, as the light had changed to green. I had passed out in my car. What the hell? I pulled the car over, then I called Brad. After about ten minutes, he came running. We hopped into my car, and he started to drive me home. "Lori, I'm really starting to get scared. What's been happening with you?", "I don't know. I feel like a different person. I think I need to speak with Steph.", "She said she is really busy. I called her after you called me. Something is weird with you. You went to see the therapist today? Right?", "Yes. But it didn't help as much.", "What exactly is going on? What did the doctor tell you?", "I have multiple personalities…", I said. Feeling like there was some truth to that. "Multiple personalities? That doesn't make any sense. You've never had anything like that before…", said Brad, looking at me while we were stopped at a stop light. "I don't know what to tell you, Brad. That's what she said.", I said, now looking at the notebook. I flipped some pages and quickly found something interesting. There was a list of Earths numbered one to eight. The way they were written suggested that there were multiple Earths, like other planets. But turning further into the notebook revealed that these Earths were in different universes. The more I looked at it, the more something started to sound off in my mind more clearly. Then, another vivid dream began.

"Stephanie, we can save Father with this…", I said, looking at Steph. She looked unsure, "And what about the other danger? The one where you said something was chasing you?", "That can be taken care of. One of my other versions figured it out. I killed her, of course. Can't have too many versions of me with this info. Anyway, we need gravitytium. Once we gain that, we can navigate the Astral World without fear.", "Gravitytium? And you're sure? Where do we get it?", "That's the hard part. From within the Earth. This substance can only be found close to the core. So, we'll have to drill. But, we'll be sacrificing…".

I woke up in my bed. Brad was sitting with me. I sat up really fast and looked for the little notebook. Brad had it in his hands and was looking at it. He noticed me, "What the fuck is this, Lori?", he asked, brandishing it at me. "An employee gave it to me.", I said, jumping out the bed and trying to snatch it, but Brad jerked it from my reach. "This is what's wrong with you…", he said, looking at the little book with horror on his face, "Is any of this true?", he asked. "Come on, some crazy guy…", "Lori, you're mentioned in here as discovering this thing.", "What does it say exactly?", I asked. Brad shook his head, "It's some notes on how to dream travel. Says that you bring something back from that place with you. Only you know what it is.", "If I knew, I wouldn't have to ask…", I said. I was becoming annoyed. My dreams were trying to tell me the truth. I just needed to sleep. Then I thought of Keith. I needed to speak with him. "I need to see the man who gave me that notebook.", I said. Brad shook his head, "You need rest.", he said, taking the notebook with him.

When I woke up, I realized Brad hadn't left the notebook. I was even more pissed now. I felt like I was finally remembering something important. My phone rang and I got up to answer it, "Lori Segrin speaking…", I said. "Hello, Lori. We need to speak. This is Husan Martin.".

HUSAN: I stepped into Stephanie's office. It looked like it did on Earth 5. But there was a picture on her desk. And the office next to her's had Lori Segrin's name on the plaque next to the door. "You couldn't just tell me that she's an NLA employee?", I asked, slightly upset that this was hidden from me. "Mr. Martin, I told you everything is need-to-know only. My sister's identity wasn't important for you on Earth 5 because she wasn't who she is here. Now, report.", "Keith Ledgewin has been hospitalized.", "Why?", asked Stephanie, making a serious face. "He had a freakout downtown. Not too far from where Ms. Segrin was having her therapy appointment.", "Do you think he tried to make contact with her?", "I wouldn't know. As far as I knew, Ms. Segrin had nothing to do with us…", I said, getting even more angry. Stephanie thought about this then reached into her desk and pulled out a familiar looking file. ReportZ. "I've seen that…", I said. "I never told you who wrote this…", "You said it was a need-to-know only situation. Do you plan on telling me now?", "It was Lori.", "WHAT?!", I yelled. This was impossible. "Boss, please tell me what the hell is going on. You brought me on back on Earth 5. Then you keep this information from me? What is happening? Do you understand how crazy it was when you told me we were going to destroy the Earth? I couldn't believe I went along with you… But now, what the fuck is this, Brady?", I asked. I was extremely pissed off. "I don't know what will happen, but show Lori ReportZ. On this Earth, we work together, so maybe something will actually trigger.", "And what do you think is happening on Earth 5 now? We've been here for nearly two months.", "Probably has gone through the worst of the cataclysms. I've been to one of the destroyed Earths. The moon is coming towards the Earth, and our bodies will be forever cut off from that universe.", "My God…", I said, staring at her in horror. "Why are you acting remorseful now, Martin? You knew people were going to die, and that you'd be alive somewhere else. Get over it. You have your family members back, right?", "Well, yes. But my uncle never met his wife, so my cousin was never born…", I said, realizing that difference held a small effect within the family on this Earth that I was born into. "So? Was he important? If so, go to another Earth, and I'll work with a different Martin.", "Is it really that easy for you? That is insane…", "Are you calling me crazy?", asked Stephanie, very menacingly. "No, I just can't understand how someone can be so cold. Those other people didn't transfer their consciousnesses. They died…", I said, "My family is suffering back there. Don't you have family back there?", "The only family I have is Lori. That's it. We had no relation back on Earth 5. But here, our mother is the same woman. We have different fathers. Enough of this. Take ReportZ to Lori. It's time I test something out…", said Stephanie, dismissing me.

CHAPTER 4

THOSE LEFT BEHIND

BRAD: When everything started, it was the most frightening thing I'd ever seen. Japan was completely wiped off the face of the Earth within three days. Storms the likes of which had only been described in the Bible were now bombarding the Earth. Me and Mara took the kids to the shelter where everyone was gathering for safety. It was raining so hard, and the wind was blowing at impossible speeds. Some people had been carried off by the wind. None of us had time to ask what was going on? It was just one thing after another. My son looked at me at one point, he was only seven, and asked, "Dad, we aren't going home, are we?". I didn't know how to answer. The last thing a parent wants to tell his child is that we're going to die. Suddenly, my son was ripped away from me, as water came flooding into the building. I had no idea where my wife or daughter had gone. This was it. We were going to die. I was going to die. I felt myself being thrown all over. Everyone else as well. I couldn't even call for my son like you see in the movies. The roof finally caved, and everyone screamed. And I knew I was dead.

"Brad...", someone said. I didn't recognize the voice. It was hot. I was hooked up to something. It was an IV. "What the...?", "Don't try to move just yet, hun. Trust me, you've been out for a while.", said a woman with sort of auburn hair. It was short and to her shoulders. She was wearing all black. It looked like a military outfit of some sort. I tried to sit up, but she forced me back down again, "Brad, listen, I'm going to tell you this now; Everything you knew is gone. And we are going to leave and go somewhere else. You need to trust me. Names Roxy. Now, just lay there for a bit, and I'll finish fixing this soup.", said Roxy. I didn't know what she meant. I suddenly started having flashes of what happened at the shelter. I tried to sit up again, and this time, I swung my legs over the table, "Where is my family?", "I'm assuming they're dead. Most people are dead. Especially if they were in that shelter incident two months ago. You've been out for two months. And there is now no contact anywhere. Signals have been jammed for weeks. Have no idea where other survivors might be. I found you. Laid up on the remains of the shelter. I brought you here and took care of you. You're welcome.", "No… My family could be alive…", "They aren't. I'm sorry. We all lost people. Best to just accept it. Who knows, where we're going, you might see them again…", "What? When we die?", "No. We're not dying. We're getting out of here. Trust me, I have a plan. It will work. We just have to hope certain people don't catch on.", "My family can't be dead…", "The roof of the shelter came crashing down. After that, everyone drowned. I saw plenty of dead bodies, and I knew your wife and kids. They were there, dead. But you were alive. So I saved you.", "NO!", I yelled, ripping the IV out of my arm, and storming outside of the place I had been in. I turned and realized it was a building protected by a huge metal fence. It was really cold outside, and I looked up and fell back. The moon was close enough that you could see the whole top of it as if looking through a telescope. I quickly ran back inside. "Yeah, you don't want to go out there. I spent years preparing this place. I knew this was going to happen. And I had to wait for it, so I could try and get off this planet.", "How…how?", I stuttered. "I can't tell you that yet. Plus, when we get ready to leave, we have to leave this place, so, yeah. You need to hurry and get better.", said Roxy, now walking off to go do something. I just sat in disbelief. Roxy had a camera that was outside, staring right at the moon. I was terrified.

Over the course of the next few days, I realized that outside was completely dangerous. There were temperature fluctuations that could kill you. Roxy was prepared for this. She specially designed suits that would allow us to weather the climate. I asked Roxy who she was before the world ended, and she said, "Someone who knew this would happen.". Roxy barely spoke, and kept busy with preparing to leave. She was tuning up a buggie looking type vehicle when I approached her and crouched, "Are you sure you saw Mara dead?", "I hate to do this.", said Roxy, getting up. She led me to a room I hadn't been inside of. The compound was basically a small mansion. I didn't understand how Roxy knew me and my family. After walking into the room, I saw it was a red room with pictures hanging on strings all crossing each other. Roxy grabbed a specific one and handed it to me. I saw Mara and my daughter, holding each other, but definitely dead. Their eyes were wide open in fear. She gave me another picture, and I saw that my son was crushed by the ceiling. I threw the pictures and broke down. "I told you to just accept it.", "I appreciate you saving me, but please, I need some alone time.", I said, not appreciating Roxy's rudeness. "No, I need your help. There's something I don't have on this compound. We have to leave to get it. We need it for the journey.",

"Okay. What is this stuff?", "Gravitytium.", "What?", "Trust me. We need it.", "I've never even heard of anything like that…", "NLA discovered it. They destroyed the Earth. We need to go to the NLA building and get it.", "It wasn't destroyed?", "There is an underground bunker where they keep the stuff.", "How do you know that, Roxy?", "I kind of used to work for them. Now get ready. You don't have time to cry.", said Roxy, leaving me. I looked at the pictures on the floor, and picked up the one with Mara on it, "I'm sorry, Mara…", I said, crying silently.

LORI: I was waiting in the parking lot of NLA. Husan Martin finally came down to talk to me. I recognized him, "You made me come here…", I said, not knowing if I should attack him or not. "Lori, you need to read this.", he said. I looked at what he handed me, and it was a file that said 'ReportZ' across the front with big letters. Now I was intrigued. I opened it, and recognized the handwriting. I wrote this;

REPORTZ:

Upon learning how to enter the Astral World through the experiment now referred to as 'Sleep Test 106', Patient 157 experienced what he referred to as a waking nightmare. A shadow figure (much like the ones mentioned in those who have experienced sleep paralysis) suddenly was following him everywhere. Upon further examination, it was seen that this shadow does not wait for its victim to be alone, but rather will attack as soon as opportunity presents itself. Patient 157 went into a coma, but soon awoke, and claimed to be the same person, but didn't have memories of certain things Patient 157 had experienced prior to the coma. It was believed he had forgotten. But I ran some tests, and noticed that the brain patterns in Patient 157 have changed drastically. I realized that he had become someone else. After spending many days with Patient 157, I finally got him to confess. He was indeed the shadow that was pursuing the original 157. I asked where the original was, and was told that he is There. 'There' meaning the Astral World. This was our ticket in. If we can navigate it, perhaps we can save our dear President, Jack Brady.

I looked at the first half of the report again, unable to accept what I'd just read. I decided to read the rest. I looked at Husan, and I turned and got into my vehicle. He didn't try to stop me as I started to drive home. Upon getting in the door, Brad was here. He had the little notebook. "What else are you hiding, Lori?", he asked. I was shocked by his demeanor. He seemed to actually be angry. "You don't believe that. Do you?", "You believe it. You think that you can save your step father with this. You're wrong. And I think you know. Something is after you. You're not my Lori. Everything I read in this thing answered a lot of questions I've had. Now I know for sure.", he said, throwing the book at me, "So, what have you done with the Lori from this Earth?", he asked, crossing his arms. I decided to tell him the full story. He thought about it, "And did you know me on this other Earth?", "Yes, but we didn't have a good relationship. Listen, I'm just as confused, but I got this...", I said, holding up ReportZ. Brad took it from me and began looking through it. I didn't want him to get further than I was in the report. I let him hold it a bit longer than I took it from him. He looked at me in shock, "Lori, you wrote that… You were experimenting on people? I knew you were hiding things…", said Brad, looking like he didn't even know me. "Where is Patient 157 now?", "He's…dead. He went into shock and just died. It was sudden.", "And you're not afraid of this happening to you? Why?", "Brad, I told you, I don't know, because I'm not the Lori from this Earth.". Brad walked out the door. I didn't know what to feel. I needed to see Keith. My phone rang, "Segrin…", "Listen closely. Someone is going to kill you. You won't get away with what you've done for much longer.", said the voice on the other end. They hung up. As I was starting to panic, I felt the presence of the shadow. I turned to face it, and it just leered at me. "Whatever you're going to do, just do it.", I said. It quickly came to me, grabbed me, I now couldn't move at all, and I saw the most horrifying thing I'd ever seen. Where originally, there was no mouth, it now had one, and the teeth were in the form of a spiral going all the way down its throat. The teeth started to move and spin, as the shadow grabbed my head and put its mouth on mine. I felt the worst pain imaginable. I couldn't break free. I tried to struggle. I screamed, as I fell to my knees, wondering why I let this happen. Then, the shadow was gone, and so was the pain. But a different type of pain started to settle in. I suddenly started seeing multiple versions of me splitting apart from my body all at once and then combining back with me. We were an amalgamation of flesh and sinew, sewing ourselves back together each time we split. I screamed a loud scream, then I woke up in the hospital.

CHAPTER 5

GRAVITYTIUM

BRAD: We got suited up, Roxy making sure there were no holes or anything in our suits, then we loaded up into the buggie she had been fixing up. Fear was coursing through me as I realized I had to go outside again. She pressed the button on her visor to open the big garage door. As it opened, the moon was just as close as ever, bearing down upon the Earth as if it were its parent, scolding it for being so close. I couldn't take my eyes off it. You could see the craters and the impact markings with the naked eye. I even saw bases on the moon. I couldn't believe it, "There really were bases up there… It wasn't just a conspiracy…", "Yeah. NLA has some bases up there, along with some other companies and of course Uncle Sam.", said Roxy, as she was pulling out of the garage. I couldn't really feel what the air felt like because of the hazmat suit. It was warm inside. As we were driving, I got to look more closely at everything. Buildings were completely decimated. It was the most horrible thing I had ever seen. There were no people, stores were either caved in, or if they were standing, they were just grim reminders of what we've lost. We were passing Mara's favorite restaurant. I was going to take her there for our anniversary in two months. I started to cry inside my suit. I could tell Roxy knew, but she was ignoring me. I couldn't believe there were no people. I noticed we were coming up on the old NLA building, and was shocked to see that it was still in good condition. NLA was written at the top of the building, with the words 'Next Level Advancements' being spelled out in smaller fonts. Roxy stopped the buggie and stepped out. I just followed her lead. We had built-in headsets, "Roxy, how do we get this gravity stuff?", "I told you, it's located in an underground bunker. This is one of NLA's biggest kept secrets, so it was buried far from the public or even those without clearance.", "And did you have clearance?", I asked Roxy. She just ignored me as she took a strange cellphone out. It had wires attached to it. She plugged it into the building's security system outside of the door. She waited, then the red light turned green, and the sliding door opened. "We couldn't have just broken the glass?", "Bulletproof glass?", answered Roxy. I could barely see her face in the suit. I was absolutely shocked once we stepped inside. There was destruction in here. There was a giant globe that used to hover above everything, but it was shattered upon the floor. Papers were thrown around everywhere. Debris from the ceiling and asbestos was all over the place. There was also a really nice looking table, but it was covered in blood. Roxy looked worried, from what I could see in her suit. "Why is that table covered in blood?", I asked. Suddenly, we heard voices. There was a big table, and Roxy grabbed my hand and we hid behind it. "Someone entered. The security for the door went down. If that happens, someone is here…", "Well, I don't see anybody. And we need to do the draw soon.", "But we won't have to if we find whoever is here! We won't need the draw!", "I know you're afraid, but we all go somewhere nice after.", "I don't believe that! I just don't want to die!", "Is that why you wanted to check?", "Outsiders are immediate sacrifices! You know that! We've only had to do the draw because there isn't anybody else! And those sons of bitches higher-ups have all gone. You read the paper. REPORTZ! They left, and we have no way of joining them because we weren't WORTHY!", "Calm down. We'll find the intruders.", said two men who were walking around the huge lobby trying to find us. Roxy was literally shaking. "You didn't expect this?", I whispered to her. She just ignored me, "We need to split up. We can't let them find us. There is a map in the corner. Go find a place to hide, and in three hours, come back here.", said Roxy, quickly darting from behind the table. "THERE!", one of the men yelled, as Roxy ran into a door. The men tried to follow her, but she had locked the door somehow. I realized this was my chance to get away. I tried to sneak from behind the table without being seen. But unfortunately, a third person entered the room. "And who are you?", they asked, pointing a gun at my head. I didn't answer. I was too afraid. "They are our sacrifice for tonight…", said one of the earlier men. "I don't think so.", said the man with the gun to my head. A woman came running out of the same office that the man had come out of, "Make him take this off.", the woman said. The man hit me with the gun, and I immediately started to remove the hazmat suit. The woman had black hair, a round face, and powdery lips. The man looked a bit rough, with scabs on his face. The other two men were similar, except they weren't as bad as the guy with the gun. "What are you doing here? How did you get in?", asked the woman. "I don't know. I was looking for shelter.", I said. "You're a fucking liar. Those doors don't just open for anybody. Do you know about the Astral Plane?", the woman asked. I just shook my head. "There was another. They ran into the meeting room and locked the door. They abandoned this person, so this person doesn't matter.", said one of the earlier men. He had a mess of black hair on his head. "He matters, because he is going to tell me who else is here…", said the woman, "Plus, Tommy would want to know.", "FUCK THAT GUY!", yelled the man with the gun. He turned and pointed it at the woman. "Harold, do you think this is wise? Remember why we let you live.", said the woman. Harold lowered his gun, then motioned for me to follow the woman. I did, but Harold still hit me with his gun.

When I woke up, it was in a different lobby, and there were other people now. At least fifty-something. I sat up quickly, as a man wearing a green dress shirt and slacks came up to me. He was bald and not that tall, four inches less than six feet, "How did you get in here? It is important to know.", he said, sweating, looking down on me nervously. The smell coming off him was pretty bad. Now that I thought about it, the whole lobby smelt pretty bad. I looked around, and it was just degeneracy; There were men and women dancing, loud music playing. Some of the men and women were nude and actually having sex in the open. There were several alcohol bottles all over the place. I looked at the man again, and this time I noticed he was holding a gun. "I'm going to ask again; How did you get in here?", he asked. The woman from earlier came and sat by me. She was wearing a business outfit and wasn't participating with the other people. "He just needs incentive. This is Tommy. He was one of our financiers. I'm Chrys. And we are the last people left in the city. We've found others and brought them here, but…", "But people have to be appeased somehow. Now, tell us how you got in here, damn it!", yelled Tommy, putting the gun on my gut. I noticed they had completely removed my hazmat suit. I was wearing the gray sweats and black shirt that Roxy had given me. "Tommy, relax. Let me take him. I promise I'll make him talk. Follow me.", said Chrys, leading me away from the strange party taking place. She led me to Stephanie Brady's office. We walked in, and the man with a gun from earlier was sitting in here. "So, you bring him in here…", "Harold, get out. You know you're not supposed to be in here.", "That other person got into the clearance only area. Just thought you should know.", said Harold, now getting up from the seat behind the desk and leaving. "Sorry about him. We're all on edge here. After all, the world has ended. What do you know about that?". I didn't know what to say. "I've lost my family.", I said, wanting to cry, but being too afraid at the moment. "Listen, I'll make you an obvious deal; I will give you the best fuck of your life if you tell me why you're really here.", said Chrys, now coming up to me, and grabbing my genitals. I grabbed her wrist and removed her hand, "I'm not interested.", I said, stepping back from her. She looked like she was thinking, "There aren't many pretty women like me in the city.", she said, smiling, and undoing the buttons on her blouse. I stopped her, "You don't have to do this…", "Tell me who you came here with… There shouldn't be anybody else able to access the clearance only area. So, who did you come here with?", "It doesn't matter. I'm pretty sure she is abandoning me.", "All the more reason to tell me. I'll tell you what I know, then you just tell me if I'm close to the reason you're here. NLA destroyed the world, and we all are going to die in a week when the moon finally collides with the Earth. But there is a way for us to survive. If we transfer our consciousness to another universe. The tech is locked away in the clearance only area. So, like, am I close?", asked Chrys. I didn't know what the fuck she was talking about. Roxy said we were going to go somewhere. She said I might see my family again. I didn't understand what she meant. "ReportZ. Do you know about it?", asked Chrys. I just shook my head. Chrys started to cry and just sat behind Stephanie's desk. She knocked everything off it and screamed. I wanted to comfort her, because I understood. "I DID EVERYTHING YOU ASKED!", she was yelling at a picture on the desk. She picked it up and started to repeatedly smash it upon the desk. I quickly came forward and grabbed her, "STOP!", I yelled. She came from around the desk and threw her arms around my neck, "Just hold me. Please...", she said, crying into my shirt. "Listen, Chrys, I understand. But this isn't going to help you.", "You won't help me, nobody else can. This building holds the last people in the city. This is it. So, if you won't say...", "Are you going to tell them?", I asked, pointing at the door. "They're crazy. Of course not. You have no idea how hard I've had to protect myself. Tommy out there is the leader of that cult, and he likes me, so I've been able to skate by. But soon, he'll expect more from me that I'm not trying to give. Please, help me. Please...", cried Chrys, falling into my chest. I felt really bad now, "I'm here for the gravitytium.", "I know where that is. I can take you to it.", "But I thought it was locked away?", "Ms. Brady has a stash. She's used it before. Let me take you to it.", "Okay, but how do we use it after?", "That person you came here with, you said she is a she? What is her name?", "Roxy.", "Roxy? There wasn't a Roxy that... Oh my god... The coma patient... The one they had experimented on... YES!", yelled Chrys, now grabbing my hand, "We're getting out of here.", she said, opening the door. I still didn't understand a damn thing.

A TALE OF MIXED PERSONALITIES

ROXY: "Don't worry, Ms. Yuling, you'll be fine. These are the best doctors in Maine. We'll take care of you.", the nice nurse said, as she walked out of my room. I was angry, but I also understood why I had to be here. I had Ataxia. Basically I couldn't function normally. I was always a bit off. I couldn't walk straight, or just properly pour things. It started a few months back. Lately it has gotten way worse, and my brother was really worried, so he booked me an appointment. Of course I learned about the Ataxia two days ago, and they have been keeping me overnight so that I don't have any accidents. But this night was one of the scariest nights. I had lived in Lewiston, and it had been my home for as long as I could recall. I never moved out of my city or state. Next Level Advancements said they could help me, but they'd have to move me to Greenville, Maine. That's where their main office was located. The woman who spoke to me was named Chrys Tinner. She was a nice lady. My brother didn't trust NLA, and didn't like the idea of me going behind his back and signing off on this. He said Stephanie Brady couldn't be trusted. "Do you work for her?", I asked, knowing my brother would never be good enough to work for NLA. I was only twenty at the time and my brother was six years older than me. He took care of me most of my life because our parents were drug addicts. When my brother turned eighteen, we went to live with an aunt. She was okay, but my brother still did most of the work in my life. I was pretty smart though, and I actually WANTED to work for NLA. The day Chrys showed up to take me back to Greenville, my brother said he wanted to stay in full contact with me. "I don't ever want to be told I can't speak with her.", he said. Chrys just smiled and said, "Of course.", as she wheeled me to her vehicle.

When we got to Greenville, it was almost immediate that the change happened. Chrys got me out of her car, then two men came and grabbed me. "Don't worry, everything will be okay.", she said, waving at me, as the men put me in the wheelchair they brought out. I was starting to get worried. But that faded once I saw Stephanie was here to greet me herself. I wished I could stand. "So, Ms. Yuling, I understand you have a certain type of mental condition.", "Ataxia. It makes it to where you can't walk straight, or do really anything straight…", I said, in absolute awe. She was gorgeous. She had blonde hair that was down past her shoulders, she was wearing a colorful business outfit, and she wore blue high-heel shoes. "Aww, that must have been horrible. Well, come with me. We'll get your healing process started.", she said, now walking behind me and pushing my chair. I felt like I was in a dream. She was walking very slowly and pushing me down a very long and cold corridor. The walls were gray and black, and there was a strange stench. I didn't understand what it was. As we got near a door, I could see my brother, Teric, on the other side of the door. "What is Teric doing here?", "Ah yes, your brother. Well, he just wanted to make sure you're taken care of.", said Stephanie, but once we got in, I saw a gun being pointed at Teric. "What…what is going on?", I asked, now getting scared again. "So, you've seen your sister.", "WHAT ARE YOU GOING TO DO TO HER!?", Teric yelled, as the man with the rifle hit Teric on the back of his head with the gun. "STOP! THAT'S MY BROTHER!", I yelled, confused. "Don't worry, Teric was under the impression we were going to kill you.", said Stephanie, laughing somewhat. She was horrible. My brother was right. "What are you going to do?", I asked nervously. "Don't worry. We've already tested this out one-hundred and fifty-seven times. You'll be fine. I just want you to find someone for me.", "I can barely walk… How do you expect me to find someone for you? That's impossible for me.", "I'm sending you somewhere you CAN walk.", said Stephanie, as the two men from before snatched me out of my wheelchair and placed me inside what appeared to be a pod. My brother fought, and eventually, Stephanie pulled out a pistol and shot him herself. "NO…!", I yelled, as I saw my brother die. "Get her prepared for the Astral Plane. I don't want to waste time with this one.", said Stephanie. Not looking at me as she left the room. The men closed the pod and I was stuck inside of it. Once again, I was scared, banging on the pod door. I felt myself beginning to pass out.

When I woke up, I didn't know where I was, but one thing was for sure, I could walk. I stood up, feeling strange. I couldn't believe it. I started to walk straight and felt like I was dreaming. Suddenly to my right, was a figure who was cloaked in shadow. I started to back away, but they caught up to me. Suddenly, I was awake inside of the pod again. "LET ME OUT! LET ME OUT!", I screamed, banging on the pod door. Then, that creepy shadow was outside my pod. Looking down on me. I saw its mouth start to open and its teeth was just a spiral going all the way down its throat. It started to spin its teeth, and bare down upon me. I screamed, then woke up in my bed. I felt like I couldn't walk again, except much worse. I also couldn't move my arms. The shadow was in the corner of my room now. Moving closer and closer. It stretched out its arms towards me and I was completely stuck. Couldn't move even an inch. As it got close to me, I suddenly remembered that stench in the corridor. It smelled like rotten eggs and bad fish. When it touched me, my skin began to burn, and even though it felt like my voice was stuck in my throat, I somehow managed to scream, "ROXY! What's wrong?", asked Teric, looking at me with worry. "TERIC!? BUT STEPHANIE SHOT YOU!", I yelled, trying to get out of the bed, but my legs wouldn't let me stand right. My brother held me, "It's okay, Rox, you just had a bad dream...", "It wasn't. I...", I didn't know what was going on. "Rox, I have to go to work, but Mara is here to look after you.", said Teric, kissing my head, then leaving. I was confused. I didn't know who Mara was, nor why she would be here to take care of me. Well, I knew why she was here to take care of me, but I never had a caretaker before. My brother handled all of that. What the hell was happening? I looked out the window and saw Mara talking to a handsome man. I had feelings for him. His name is Brad. What the fuck? How did I know that? Something was wrong. Mara turned to come in, and I saw that Brad was leaving. Something in me didn't want him to. I also had the urge to see Stephanie, even though she murdered my brother in front of me. But...did she? He was alive. I'm alive right now. Where the hell am I? Mara entered my room, "Are you hungry, Roxy?", she asked with that slightly English accent she has. "Um, sure.", I said. She smiled and went to go fix my food. I came down using my wall slider, and when I got down, I noticed everything was different here. There was a picture of me and Teric, and there was a man in the picture. He's my uncle. But Teric and I lived with our aunt... "Waffles this morning?", asked Mara, making waffles from scratch. "Mara, I'm sorry, but when did you first start working here?", I asked. Mara just laughed, "Is that what we're doing today?", she said, pouring me some orange juice. I sipped it, and it tasted normal, but everything else was out of place. I felt a presence, and saw the shadow. I screamed and pointed at it, and Mara just gave me a really confused look, "Roxy, your brother said you're not feeling well. Maybe you should lie back down, love.", "No, I can't. Something isn't right, Mara. Why are you with Brad?", I asked, not even knowing where that was coming from. "Brad? My boyfriend? What about him?", "I mean...", I didn't know what to say at this point. I had said something stupid, and now I just wanted to get away. The shadow had disappeared.

CHAPTER 7

BRAD'S DECISION

ROXY: I hated leaving Brad like that, but he'll be okay. I had to get the gravitytium. It was well hidden down below. I had found the elevator that takes you down to the clearance only area of the building. Luckily everything was running on back-up power. But in a week's time, we'd all be dead from the moon crashing into us. I couldn't think about that though. I had to use what I knew to survive. It was the only way to get revenge, and possibly go somewhere where my brother wasn't shot by Stephanie Brady. As I moved further down the corridor, my nostrils were hit with the smell of rotting eggs and sour fish. I saw the shadow waiting for me down the corridor. "NO! STAY AWAY!", I yelled, now turning to run the other direction. The shadow never had to run. Somehow just walking, it was fast enough to catch me. More like it was gliding. But I knew what to do. I took out my taser, taking my arms from out of the hazmat sleeves and bringing my hands inside the suit. I saw the shadow getting closer, and I stunned myself. The shadow made a weird gurgling noise before it disappeared, "I've got to hurry.", I said, now running the original way I was going before.

BRAD: Chrys was leading me out of the office, when Tommy appeared at the door. He pointed the gun at me and Chrys, "What were you two doing?", "Talking. I'm taking Brad to something that could save us all. You just have to be patient.", said Chrys, putting her hand on Tommy's face. For a second he looked like he was about to give in, then he hit Chrys with the gun. She fell on the floor, and then Tommy pointed the gun at me, "You're trying to take her from me. I won't let you…", "TOMMY, THIS ISN'T YOU! THINK ABOUT IT!", I yelled. I didn't know Tommy, but I don't believe he's been the person he is showing me now all his life, "You're a good guy. And Chrys says you have to trust her. She's got you this far…", I said. Tommy was thinking, "Yes… But she hasn't allowed me to make love to her.", "It's coming. We have to get out of here, Tommy. It's dangerous.", said Chrys, rubbing her face, but there was a bump coming up. "So you're going to get me out of here?", asked Tommy, still pointing his gun at me. "Yes.", I lied. Tommy bought it, and allowed me to help Chrys off the ground. I could see Chrys was about to attack Tommy, and I didn't think that was wise. "Chrys, lead the way.", I said, to get her to turn away from that idea. "Okay…", she said, giving a really bad side-eye to Tommy. I allowed Chrys to walk ahead and decided to press Tommy for info. Maybe it was time I started trying to understand. "Tommy, help me understand this… What happened?", I asked. Tommy was lazily pointing the gun at me now, "Lori and her fucking sister, that's what happened.", "Lori? Lori who?", I asked. The Lori I knew was a terrible person. I dated her in college. She broke my heart by sleeping with one of our professors. Then she continued to gaslight me into thinking it was my fault. Then she got her own mother to kill herself. Sadly, her mother survived. On top of that, from what I understood, she killed her step-father, but he may have been abusive. I don't know how much of Lori was fake and how much was real. "Lori Segrin. Yeah, here she didn't have anything to do with the company. But every other Earth…", "Wait, what do you mean every other Earth?", "Every other Earth, she is the VP of NLA.", said Chrys, still angry from when Tommy hit her. We walked up to the other doors opposite the ones that Roxy ran into. Once the door was opened, I saw it was just a meeting room. We all walked in and Chrys closed the door, then quickly picked up a clipboard and started to beat Tommy with it over his head. He tried to fight her, but I grabbed his gun, which slipped right out of his hand. Tommy started to cower towards the wall. "Shoot him.", said Chrys, with a sadistic smile on her face. "No.", I said, taking out the clip and throwing the bullets. I helped Tommy stand then punched him. He shook his head, "Tell me about Lori… Everything and anything you can…".

TOMMY: "Okay, I will. Just don't kill me. Lori and I were trying to prevent the end of the world. I thought she was a good person. A journalist I could trust to stop this from happening. But instead, she turned out to be connected. Once everyone was gone, we raided this place. And Chrys here found ReportZ. It told us everything we needed to know. For years, Stephanie had been experimenting on the mentally ill. Stealing them from their families under the guise she was going to cure them. And of course those families believed her. Those poor people were tortured. And the worst was in the beginning. Forcing them to sleep, injecting them with all kinds of chemicals, moving them like cattle, branding them. The last one, she was a fighter. She woke up and escaped out of the hospital where they placed her.", "Roxy. The girl you came in here with.", said

Chrys, angry that I was still breathing. "Wait, Roxy was experimented on? That's why she knows this place…", "Wrong. She's never been here before, Brad. That's what I was trying to tell you in the office. She has knowledge of this place. And if ReportZ is true, it came from the Astral Plane. That girl has been to another universe and back.", said Chrys. "But that sounds fucking crazy. You guys believe this?", asked Brad. He was looking like he was going to die now. "That's why she's here. She needs the…", Chrys got quiet. "Needs the what?", I asked. "Shut up, Tommy. You're still in hot water. Now, those people partying out there, will they try to kill us if they catch us?", asked Brad. I just smiled, "They're longing for it.", I said, feeling blood come down my head, "Let's cut the shit. You knew Lori.", "Yeah. I knew her. She's dead now right? Like everyone else.", "No. Her body is on the moon. She has left for another universe. Because she was Stephanie's stepsister. Not here, but on every other Earth. The Stephanie that took over OUR Stephanie wasn't that Stephanie. Pretty much, our Stephanie didn't know anything about the Astral Plane, until she was taken over by a different version of herself. Then somehow she got ReportZ sent to all the universes. Lori is the full mastermind behind this. And she got lost on the Astral Plane. The real Lori is on a different Earth, braindead. Unable to wake up. And that's why Stephanie has been experimenting on people. Further. I tried to stop it. That's why she left me here…", said Chrys, starting to cry. We were all shocked that she left her. They were pretty close. But if it was a different Stephanie, then that makes sense. Brad was looking harshly at the floor. He bent down and picked up an empty syringe. He looked around the room. He walked over to the white board in the room. He then started to draw something with the needlepoint on the white board. "Do you see this? This is the problem.

See, if what you're saying is true, then I just made a work of art.", he said, laughing. "You're going mad.", said Chrys, shaking her head. I quickly ran out the room and ran back to my people, "EVERYONE! CHRYS HAS BETRAYED US AS WE KNEW SHE WOULD! SHE IS TRYING TO MATE WITH A FORBIDDEN OUTSIDER! THEY ARE TO BE SACRIFICED!", I said, and everyone quickly ran. Some people had put some clothes on, but it was more like tattered rags at this point. I'm never getting out of here. But neither are Brad and Chrys.

ROXY: As I was coming up on the door that had the gravitytium behind it, I realized that it was sealed and wasn't connected to the backup generators. "Damn…", I said, thinking if there was another way. "I could get that door open for you.", said Harold. I glared at him, "You're not supposed to be able to get down here…", I said, backing up. "Oh, Roxy, you just thought you'd waltz right in here, and take the gravitytium? Stephanie expected this… She said you stole something that isn't yours.", "That's her fault.", I said, taking out my taser, and pointing it towards Harold, "Now, just stop!", I yelled. "That thing all you got?", he asked, pulling out his gun he had earlier pointed at Brad. "I'll make a deal with you… I want to leave. Get me outta me here. Let me take the place of that Brad. He's boinking Chrys. She worked fast on him.", "That's a fucking lie.", "Oh, that's right. You like that bloke. Well, let me tell you, he ain't worth it. Now, get me to the transfer station.", said Harold, pointing his gun at me. I felt like I had no choice.

CHAPTER 8

LORI'S AWAKENING

BRAD: I went to visit this Keith guy in the hospital. I figured maybe he'd answer the questions that Lori wasn't. As I walked in, I looked around, the usual people were just sitting down in the lobby, as well as the nurses who were busy walking around. "Brad, what are you doing here?", asked one of the nurses. I was a medication technician. I delivered medication to all the hospitals. It was a cozy job that allowed me to meet Mara. A woman I had been secretly seeing behind Lori's back. She didn't know, but I was planning on leaving her. I was sick of the lies kept between her and her sister. And whatever weird experiments they had going on, it was endangering people, according to that little notebook. Then there was that ReportZ. It literally said they were experimenting on people. I had to learn what was going on. "I'm here to see a patient, Keith Ledgewin. "We've been told nobody is allowed to see him unless you have proper clearance.", said Mara, looking at me strangely. "How is that girl you've been taking care of?", "Roxy is still in a coma. Her brother doesn't know what to think. But he's had NLA people showing up at his house asking to try a safe but experimental procedure that might wake her up.", "NLA? No, they can't be trusted.", "This is about Lori?", asked Mara. "Of course it is. I can't trust her. But let's not talk about her here.", "Brad? What are you doing here?", asked Lori, walking up behind me. "Hello, Lori.", "Um, yeah, who are you again?", "Mara Hill. I'm a friend of Brad's. We've met…", "Is there something going on between you two?", asked Lori, sort of like she knew already. "Lori, I'm here to see Keith.", "No, you don't have the authority. You're not family, nor are you a coworker. You only know him from what I told you today.", said Lori, looking very angrily at Mara, "Now, don't change the subject.", "Lori, I'm glad you're here already. Now, let's go check in on Mr. Ledgewin.", said Stephanie, walking Lori away. Lori looked back, and I didn't like the look she gave me. "You need to just tell her the truth.", "Mara, I want to, believe me. But… Lori and Stephanie are powerful.", I said, now thinking if maybe I should just mind my own business.

STEPHANIE: Me and Lori walked into Keith's room, "Lori, we have more important shit than you and Brad. Tell me ReportZ helped jog SOMETHING in your memory.", she said, looking at me sadly. "Yes. I remember a lot. Even the part where I had to kill a part of myself. One of the other me's. It's fine. Not a big deal. Anyway, Keith is in a coma because he hasn't accepted his shadow. Once you accept it, it makes you powerful. You have all the knowledge all the other you's possess.", "Lori, what about Father?", "This is bigger than Father. Steph, have you accepted your shadow?", asked Lori, looking at me gravely. "Well, I used the gravitytium. And you were supposed to use it too…", "I'm sure I was given it like the rest.", "Then why didn't it work for Keith? Why is his shadow pursuing him?", I asked. Lori knew EVERYTHING about this. She discovered it. "That is quite simple; It is because this isn't his first travel.", "What?", I asked, confused, "Lori, you told me that gravitytium stops the shadows.", "Yes, but only if they don't get a hold of you prior. If any part of a shadow got to you before the gravitytium, then the shadow will haunt you for the rest of your days. You'd probably need a steady dose of GT just to live a normal life. And we both know the process to gain it. Listen, I've been thinking, if we keep trying to save Father, we'll just have to keep destroying Earth's. I have a much better plan now. Using the Astral Plane, of course. It allows us to travel to different moments. We can pull a Jack from one of those moments, and fuse his memory. It would be a bit different from having flesh and blood Jack, but it would be him. And Keith just volunteered.", said Lori. I thought about it, "How would that work?", "I can handle it, Steph. Just trust me.", "What about Harold? We left him back there. And we told him we'd bring him. You weren't even yourself on the last Earth.", "Roxy will bring him. Trust me. She'll get him here. But we need to get her body. When she wakes up, we can't let her get free. She has my memories somehow, and I still haven't figured out how. But we'll fix that. Don't worry, everything is going according to plan.".

BRAD: I was confused as to what I should think. Mara and I had walked outside. I knew it wasn't a good idea to be so open with her, but I wasn't afraid any more at the moment. I was ready to tell Lori. Plus, I really didn't think she'd care. That's when Chrys was approaching me. Chrys was Stephanie's assistant. "Brad…", she said, looking at me with a look of longing. I'd never really had much connection with her. "I need to talk to you. Privately. Please. It's important. We have to get Roxy out of this hospital. She isn't safe.", "Chrys, I believe you…", "I'm quitting my job. Now, I'm going to use what's left of it to help you. You saved my life.", she said, and I was confused. She went into the hospital. I just looked at Mara, not knowing what to think. "What the hell is she talking about?", I asked. Mara shook her head.

CHRYS: I saw Stephanie's car here, and I knew she was here for Keith. I don't know what she had planned for him, but Roxy was the more important one. She was in a coma here. And I knew why. Because this is the Earth that she woke up on. Her brother is still alive here, and she wants to get back here. I'm going to make sure everything is ready for when her and Brad arrive. If they made it back to her compound that is. Harold was after them, and he's trying to get here too. Stephanie told him things, so he knew exactly what to do. He knew how to get into the clearance only area. That son of a bitch was hiding things. So was I, I guess. I needed to get to Roxy's room, and I had memories of the Chrys from this Earth. It was like Lori said; Your consciousness fully merges. I quickly got into Roxy's room. She was hooked up to the usual machines associated with being in a coma. I took her out of her bed and placed her in the wheelchair near her bed. I then grabbed her IV and started to push her. I had to get her out of here without Lori or Stephanie noticing me. Hopefully Brad was still waiting outside. I know this Brad doesn't know me, but hopefully his mistrust of Lori is strong. On this world, Lori works with Stephanie. So it was imperative to hurry this process up. I wheeled Roxy outside, thankfully nobody stopped me. Brad was sitting in his car, and the woman he was with earlier was with him. As I took Roxy out of her chair and placed her in the backseat, Brad was looking confused, "Why are you…?", he was starting to ask. "No time. Drive. Somewhere safe. Please.", I said, looking frightfully back at the hospital.

KEITH: I woke up in the hospital. I didn't know how I got here, but I remembered being attacked by the shadow. I focused on what was in the room, and saw Stephanie and Lori. "What…?", I said, immediately sitting up. "Relax, Mr. Ledgewin. We're going to take care of you. I've been waiting for you to wake up.", said Lori, giving me a smile I didn't like too much. "I just want to go home.", "You'll get to go home, Mr. Ledgewin. But first, I want you to do me and Steph a favor.", "No, I'm not doing anything. You got your memories, didn't you?", I asked, now becoming sad. They weren't going to let me out of this room. They were going to use me somehow. Lori was smiling harder now, while Steph was just waiting patiently. "Please…", I said, looking hard at Lori. "You remember Jack, right? I want you to find him on the Astral Plane.", "YOU DO IT! I'M DONE!", I yelled, trying to force myself off the bed, but I was too weak. "Is everything okay here?", asked a nurse who poked her head in. "Everything is fine. Thank you.", said Steph, now closing and locking the door. Lori took out a device, "Let's help you get to sleep, shall we?", she said, trying to connect her rectangular device to my head with the connectors that were coming from it. I tried to run, but fell off the bed. Lori bent down and put the connectors on my temples. I tried to fight back, but Lori wasn't letting me go. I felt myself drifting, and saw the shadow coming for me. I couldn't move. I was laying on my stomach, basically foaming at the mouth in fear. I couldn't even scream for help. I was shaking, trying my hardest to move. The shadow bent down and I saw its teeth starting to spin in its now visible mouth. I screamed a silent scream in my head as I felt myself fading.

LORI: If I was correct, then the shadow has consumed Keith's mind by now. I waited, with bated breath, to see if my hypothesis was correct.

I needed to study him in full, but he should have Jack's mind by now. I purposefully searched the AP for Jack's brain waves, as soon as I learned how to read them. I looked at Stephanie. She looked lost, "Should we put him back in the bed?", she asked. I bent down to check his pulse. He was breathing. I tried to lift him on my own, but he was pretty heavy. Steph came and helped me. We put him on the bed, and he was still knocked out. "What are you expecting, Lori?", "That Jack is in his mind now. Or rather his mind belongs to Jack. It should anyway...", I said, looking hard at Keith's face. "Ms. Brady? There is an issue.", said a doctor who was opening the door with the key. "What issue?", "Apparently someone wheeled out Ms. Yuling.", "Excuse me?", said Stephanie. I got angry right away. "Get Harold on that right now.", I said, and Stephanie made the call.

CHAPTER 9

THE CRAZIES

BRAD: Chrys and I ran as fast we could towards the offices on the other side. I guess those were the manager's offices. We tried to run into an office, but the people were fast on our tails. I quickly grabbed Chrys and threw her ahead of me. She ran into an office and was waiting for me. I ran up to the door, closed it, and turned to face all the crazy fucks. I pointed the empty gun at them, and they just started to laugh. "STAY THE FUCK BACK! I'LL FUCKING SHOOT! I'M SERIOUS!", I yelled. "IT ISN'T LOADED!", yelled Tommy, and they all grabbed me. I felt like they were tearing me apart, as they were just pulling on whatever they could. I felt small cuts starting to make their way onto my body as I was being tossed around. "HOLD!", said Tommy, and all the people just stopped. They dropped me on the floor. I didn't understand how Tommy had this kind of control of this many people. "Now, do you think you've saved that stupid bitch?", asked Tommy, leaning in front of me. "What the fuck is all this for, Tommy?", "We're all going to leave this plane when we die. And then we'll go there... To the Astral Plane. But we'll be dead, won't we? We need someone like you to help us get to the pods. We could all live. But do you and Chrys only want that for yourselves? You were working with her the whole time! Confess!", yelled Tommy, and all the people cheered. I understood now. I remember Chrys said some of these people were survivors off the street. I stood up, "I can take you, but just you, Tommy.", I said. "He thinks we're fucking stupid.", someone said, and I felt a knife slash at my back. It hurt, but I still just stood there. Hoping these crazy clowns weren't going to kill me. I felt like I believed in this other Earth. Mara could be there, with my kids. I wanted to go there. I wanted my family back. "Hm… I know what to do with this fuck… Go get the wires. We're going to crucify him. Then Chrys will come looking for him. Where is Harold?", said Tommy. Everyone started to look around. "That son of a bitch. Whatever. Take him to the lobby and hang him on the piller that's still standing. We'll make it off this planet.", said Tommy, punching me.

ROXY: I was walking with Harold on my tail. We got to the door override and I opened the box. "So, tell me, are they expecting you over there?", "They're expecting you, too, Roxy. You're going to be very vital to they're plans.", "Is that right?", I asked, as I was plotting on how to get out of this situation. I still had to go get Brad. "Listen, Roxy, you better get that door open quickly.", said Harold, now putting the gun directly on the back of my head. "It's almost done. If you shoot me though, who will open this for you?", I asked. He lowered the gun, "You're right, there are other things I can do to you… So, hurry up.", he said, putting the gun on my ass and caressing it with it. I quickly started trying to figure out which wires worked. Something in my mind felt like Harold wasn't going to hurt me though. Like he NEEDED me alive. And in good condition. I felt like he was still working for Stephanie. Even through all of this. I finally heard the door clink open in the distance. "Good, now get walking.", he said, and I quickly stabbed the hand he was using to point the gun at me. He screamed and dropped the gun. I stupidly didn't try to pick it up. I just ran. I ran all the way to the door, and hit the failsafe to close it. I heard the gun fire in the distance. I had closed the door just in time. I couldn't hear Harold on the other side. I turned around, and saw the drill. This is where they destroyed this Earth. All for the stuff in the brown barrels behind me. Gravitytium. I looked down the hole, it was massive. I was above it, behind a big gigantic wall of safety glass, as well as the brown barrels that were all over the room. Not all of them had the substance in them. The ones that had the big 'G' on them were the ones that were full. I needed to do the extraction carefully. I had brought enough syringes just in case. I also knew there were pods here, so if Brad and I had to use the ones here, we could, but it was safer to get back to the compound. There were security cameras here. I saw Harold back at the door's box, trying to get it open. The failsafe button won't allow it to open unless I press it again. I was safe for now. Plus I knew the other way out. If Harold knows too, it doesn't matter. He can either wait, and hope I don't go that way, or I'll go that way, and he'll still be waiting, unsure. I quickly started to extract the gravitytium. I filled up four syringes. I thought about it then decided to fill three more. Now that I had this, it was time to go get Brad. As I was making my way to the elevator, something started to automatically play, "...as if the subject has no idea. I believe that the subject in question is Jack Brady. Studying the brainwaves of this particular shadow shows it contains memories of Jack Brady. It's a good thing I built this machine that allows me to read astral projections. If this is indeed Jack, we need a test subject that we can use to… NO, DON'T OPEN THAT! Damn it, GET HIM OUT OF THERE! Wait! The shadow is going for him. I understand that, but let's see what happens. Oh my god... Shut everything down... NOW!", yelled someone's voice. I didn't recognize the voice, but on the camera, I recognized the person. It was me. I didn't remember this. It was while I was blacked out. There was a time where I was blacked out and when I woke up, I didn't remember anything. Lori must have been controlling me. And with the experiments she had performed on other Earths, she knew how to find her step father on the Astral Plane. But what happened in the video afterwards, I don't know. Everything went black and the footage just stopped.

BRAD: I was hung up by my arms and tied to a pillar in the lobby. The crazies were each taking turns leaving marks on my body. I didn't think it could get worse. They hadn't been able to get to Chrys at least. I didn't even know her, but I risked my life for her. I felt dumb now that I knew I was going to die in a really bad way. I kept wondering if Roxy got what she came for already and left. Tommy approached me, "Still don't want to take us?", he asked. I just ignored him and stared at the floor. Somehow he got my wallet. He opened it and saw the family picture I kept there. "If only your wife knew how you so easily moved on...", he said, ripping the picture to pieces in front of me. I hated Tommy. All the other people were back to doing what they were doing before. Tommy pulled out a knife and held it to my neck, "I'll give you another chance. But you have to bring Chrys to me. After that, I'll let you leave. How's that sound?", "You sound insane. We're all going to die.", "You don't know what WE know! The Astral Plane is where ALL souls go! If I killed you with this knife, RIGHT NOW, your soul will go to the Astral Plane. Do you know what the Astral Plane is, BRAD?! It's HELL! WE opened a portal to HELL! All to bring back Jack Brady. And they found him. Oh yes, they found him, and they released DEMONS!", yelled Tommy, nicking my face with the knife and laughing hysterically. I was tired of hearing this. I just wanted this to end. Then, I saw that Harold guy coming. "Tommy, what the hell have you done with this guy? We fucking need him…", said Harold, cutting me down off the pillar. I fell onto the floor hard. "Where the hell were you?", asked Tommy. "I was trying to get the other person. Where is Chrys?", asked Harold. "She betrayed us. She was trying to mate…", Tommy was saying, but Harold hit him with his gun. The people stopped and looked. Harold shot his gun up at the ceiling, "ENOUGH! LOOK, WE HAVE A REAL CHANCE OF GETTING OUT OF HERE! THIS GUY IS THE BAIT!", yelled Harold, kneeling down, lifting my head, and holding the gun under my chin, "Isn't that right, Brad? After all, Lori does want to see you…", "What the fuck? How…? Nevermind…", I said, no longer confused about Lori's connection. Maybe there really IS a way out of all this craziness and I just need to fight back.

ROXY: As I exited the elevator that took you to my secret office, I found Chrys sitting in here crying. "Well, well, well. Look what we have here…", I said, grabbing a piece of glass that was on the floor at my feet. "Roxy…", she said, standing, "It is you…right? Not Lori Segrin?", she asked, looking frightfully at the glass shard in my hand. "Either way, I'm going to kill you…", "I'M THE REASON YOU REMEMBERED!", yelled Chrys. I thought for a minute, "Explain…", "You were being controlled fully by Lori's consciousness. I felt bad for you, so I injected you with a second dose of Gravitytium. It allowed you to gain your mind back…", said Chrys. "So, I owe my awakening to you?", "I just wanted to help. I tried to stop them…", "Okay, what do you want?", "I want to go where they went… I want out of this hell…". Did Chrys deserve this? She did help kill a lot of people, but she was sort of forced to. And based on what Harold told me, they were waiting for me to transfer my consciousness. I needed someone from here who could save me, and Chrys has before. "Okay, here.", I said, giving her one of the syringes, "You know where the pods are. Now you have what you need.", I said. She started to cry and hugged me, "You have to save Brad. Tommy had him.", "Okay, I will. Just get out of here. Save my body.", "I will.", said Chrys, now taking the elevator back down, but to the pod room. I guess I had to save Brad now.

CHAPTER 10

OVER THE MOON

BRAD: I was waiting for whatever Harold was expecting. He was sitting by me with the gun, while he had everyone else on lookout duty. I didn't understand. Tommy was whimpering. Harold had tied him up with the same wire they used to hang me off the pillar. All of a sudden, there was an Earthquake. There hadn't been one in a while according to what Roxy told me. Everyone was panicking and running around. "DON'T LOSE FOCUS!", yelled Harold, but nobody was listening at this point. I seized this opportunity to try and wrestle the gun away from him. I did, but he had another gun in the back of his pants. He shot me and the bullet hit my side. Nothing fatal, luckily. I shot back at him, and hit his shoulder. He went down, and I just thought to use the commotion to get away. I looked up towards where I had sent Chrys, and saw Roxy looking down into the lobby hard. I started waving, and she started signaling for me to get to her. The Earthquake was revving up and not calming down. The ceiling was falling apart. "It's time to go.", said Roxy, indicating she had another way out other than through the front. "Roxy, wait…there was…a woman…", "She's safe. Don't worry. We need to worry about ourselves.", said Roxy, leading me back into that same office. There was an elevator in here. As we were getting in, Harold burst through the door, firing his gun at us, as he tried to get a good footing, but the room was moving too much. The elevator doors closed and Roxy noticed I was shot. I didn't notice, but I was losing a good amount of blood. I slid down the wall to the floor. Roxy quickly reached into her bag and pulled out a first aid kit. "This isn't going to hold. We need to get you to the compound and get to the pods quickly.", she said, as she wrapped a bandage around my abdomen. Once we reached the bottom, or wherever we were going, Roxy heaved my arm across her shoulder and started to try to help me walk. She looked at all the cuts on my body and started to cry, "I'm so sorry…", she said, as I noticed there was an emergency exit. As we got near to it, a gunshot sounded off behind us, and we saw Harold, limping, but still pursuing us. "GIVE IT UP!", he yelled, firing at us, but constantly missing because of the Earthquake. The door opened by us pushing the bar down. "Brad, I can't carry you anymore.", Roxy said, buckling under my weight. I took my arm from around her, but was still really dizzy. "WE HAVE TO GET TO THE HUMVEE!", yelled Roxy, and I didn't know how I was going to get there on my own. I then saw that the emergency door opened, and Harold was coming out, but Tommy was with him. Tommy started to fight Harold, and Harold wasted no time in shooting Tommy in the head. He quickly tried to come after us, and I took out the gun I took from him and shot, but the Earth was still moving, so I missed. Roxy had already run for the humvee, and I was left behind again. This time it was just to wait for Roxy, who I trusted was coming this time. In the meantime, I was locked in a standoff with Harold, who was holding onto the wall of the building, while I was trying to stand on my own, but quickly succumbing to the blood loss and dizziness. Roxy finally was coming and she didn't stop as she ran head on into Harold with her humvee. Harold tried to jump, but the Earth made it hard. His foot got caught under the tire. He screamed, and Roxy backed up, "GET IN!", she yelled at me. I was still worried about Chrys, but didn't have time anymore. We started to ride back towards the compound. But things were getting really bad. I looked up, and saw debris was piercing the atmosphere. "That doesn't look good…", I said, as little meteors started to pelt the Earth and somewhat complicated our path to the compound. "The moon is about to crash sooner than predicted… We need to hurry.", said Roxy, driving much faster.

We finally saw the compound coming up, and relief was setting in, because I fully believed in the pod idea. I had no choice. It was either that, or just die here when the moon crashes. We heard a car behind us, and couldn't believe Harold had got some of the cult people to drive him. They were howling and yelping as they were catching up to us. "We CANNOT let them get into the comp…", Roxy was saying, then the ground split. We got lucky as the road turned up and we were now driving down a hill. We also saw a huge wave in the distance coming this way. "How in the world… We weren't near any…", "Never seen a doomsday scenario show? This is par for the course. The moon is out of control, so are the tides.", said Roxy, as we were finally pulling into the compound, which itself was also damaged. The roof had caved in. Roxy rushed in. I limped out of the humvee to follow her in. We went to her pods, which were still in good condition. "They're going to get in here. We need to hurry. Come here.", said Roxy, taking a syringe out of her bag, turning on the pods, which made a strange whirring noise, then quickly plunging the syringe into my arm and shooting the gravity stuff in there. I didn't feel anything. "Get into the pod.", she said. I did, not knowing what else to do. Then, there was the unmistakable sounds of Harold and the cult getting in here. I didn't see if Roxy got into her pod. I saw Harold standing over my pod. His gun pointed down, but then there was a loud boom. Everything went dark.

"Brad...? BRAD!", someone was yelling in my ear. I smelt a familiar perfume, and felt a familiar touch. I opened my eyes, and saw Mara. Looking down on me with worry. I was lying in bed. I quickly sat up, looked around, and recognized where I was. This was Mara's apartment. I hadn't been here in years, considering we had a house together. Mara was watching me as if she thought I was sick. "Mara... Is it really you?", I asked, and she just nodded. I quickly hugged her and kissed her. I couldn't believe it, "Am I dead?", "I don't think so...", said Mara, with a smile on her face. Chrys poked her head into the room, "Oh, good. You're awake. So is Roxy. She's downstairs.", said Chrys. I stood up, "Wait, what?", I asked. I felt like my adventure was just a dream at this point. I was expecting my children to come greet me, but looking around the room, this is exactly what Mara's room was like before we started dating. Something was completely off. Roxy finally walked into the room, "Brad, do you remember getting into the pod?", she asked, and I nodded. "We made it.", she said, crying now. There was a knock at the door, "Roxy, that's your brother. I told him you were here.", said Chrys, and Roxy practically glided to the door. "Brother? She has a...? Wait...", I said, looking out the window. There was no giant moon in the sky. Just the sun. How it's supposed to be.

ROXY: I went to the door, and Teric was indeed standing there. He looked shocked when he saw me walking normally and standing on my own. "They cured you…", he said, still in shock. "Sure, in a way.", I said, unable to contain myself. I hugged my brother. I was so happy that he was alive. I pulled him into the house, looked around, then closed the door. Everyone else came downstairs. "Good, now, we need to talk about how we're going to kill Lori and Stephanie.", I said, and Brad and Mara looked nervous, but Chrys was on board. "Yes, if we don't, they'll just do the same thing.", "Oh, no, they'll do much worse. I know what the Astral Plane is now. It's one of the gateways to Hell. Lori, using me, opened a portal to Hell. She didn't know back then, but she does now. And if that portal gets opened again, it won't just stop at this Earth, it will go for the rest. We have to stop them…".

LORI: Keith finally opened his eyes. "About time. How do you feel?", I asked. Keith stood up, "Steph…? Lori?", he said. "Daddy?", asked Stephanie, and Keith smiled, "You girls are something else. But, you really should have left me where I was…", "Why? What do you mean?", I asked, not understanding. He quickly grabbed Stephanie by her throat and snapped her neck. "WHAT HAVE YOU DONE!?", "You can find her the same way you found me, Lori. As a matter of fact, you're going to do us ALL a favor.", said Keith, his eyes turning red. I backed away, "What are you?", "You summoned me, Lori. Now you'll bring the rest.", Keith said, slapping me. I passed out.

CHAPTER 11

GATE TO HELL

BRAD: "I contain a portion of Lori Segrin's memory. She tried to possess me on the Astral Plane. She failed because Chrys saved me by giving me an extra dose of gravitytium. It was enough for me to gain my mind back and take over. Now I just have Lori's memories, and some of the stuff I know, I learned while Lori was controlling me. Her and her sister want to bring back their father, Jack Brady. He died though. But Lori believed his essence was somewhere on the Astral Plane. They just had to find it, then provide a vessel. But the Astral Plane isn't just some place we go when we sleep. It's our literal souls that are departing our body and traveling the Astral Plane. You know what else lives on the Astral Plane?", "Demons. Tommy said something about that.", "Exactly. Demons who want our souls. So, when Lori started sending test subjects, they started consuming them. But once Lori had all she needed, she stopped. And the demons didn't like that. So, they want her to keep the portal opened, so in short...", "They can overrun the Earth. Yeah, we need to stop them.", I said, believing every word of this. There was a part of me that has been living on this Earth for twenty-seven years. And at the same time, I just escaped an apocalypse where the moon crashed into the Earth. I was sold. Mara felt like she couldn't hear anymore and stepped away. Roxy's brother looked confused, but she had explained to him what was going on. I went to sit next to Mara. In this world, we were seeing each other behind Lori's back. But I was ready to confess this. I could feel all these emotions all at once. Mara looked at me like she wasn't sure, but I placed my hand on her hand and she smiled. She turned on her television, and I couldn't believe the headline, 'CEO Jack Brady's daughter found in hospital patients room with neck snapped'. There was a body in a body bag, and the reporter was mentioning that Lori was with her, but seems to have gone, and nobody has seen her. "We were just there with both of them…", said Mara, looking at me with fear in her eyes. She was realizing we were right. "Stephanie is dead, and nobody knows where Lori is…", I said, walking back into the other room where Chrys was watching Roxy's brother, Roxy was looking at me in shock, and Roxy's brother just looked like he was ready for whatever we were going to do. "I know where she is. Where they are. If I'm right, she stupidly placed the demon inside of Keith. We need to get to the Astral link room at NLA headquarters.", said Roxy, standing, "And we're going to need weapons.", she said, looking at her brother. "Oh, we can go get weapons.", he said, smiling from ear to ear. Mara approached me, "PLEASE BE CAREFUL!", she said, kissing me. I never thought I'd feel this again. I held her tight, "Don't worry. I'm coming back. There are things you and I have to do.", I said, looking at her stomach. Mara blushed, but she let me go. Me, Roxy, and her brother left Chrys and Mara behind.

LORI: We were standing in the room below NLA headquarters. The place where we kept the Astral Portal. I didn't know what to think. I was terribly wrong about the Astral Plane. I just got my sister killed. I didn't know what to do, but the possessed Keith wanted me to open the portal to free more of his friends. "Now, Lori, go ahead.", he said, as I stood in front of the activator. I quickly pulled my gun I had hidden, "No, I'm not doing it.", I said, shooting him. When I shot him, the bullet went in, but Keith didn't even move, and these strange symbols appeared all over his body. He slapped me again, and I flew into some empty barrels. "DO YOU THINK THIS IS A GAME, LORI?! OPEN THE DAMN PORTAL!", he yelled. I tried shooting him again, crying as I did so, but nothing was working. He approached me, picked me up by the back of my neck, made me walk back to the control panel, and slammed my face into it multiple times. He then let me fall to the floor. "Fine, I'll do it…", he said, activating the doorway. But he needed me to put my password for the doorway to activate. He looked down on me, "You disappoint me, Lori Segrin. To find Hell, and to discard it. You could have been a queen down there…", said the demon. "What makes you think I'd want that?", "That's all you've ever wanted. To be special. Isn't that why you killed Jack Brady? Oh, you think I don't know? You come from a different Earth. All the Earths are connected. That's how we found you. We showed you.", "You TRICKED ME?!", I yelled, unable to accept the reality of what was happening. Then the door opened, and in came Roxy, Brad, and her brother. It didn't surprise me that Roxy knew how to get in here. The demon waved his hand and the three of them flew into the walls. I had done a lot of stupid things in my life, but summoning a demon was a new low. Getting my sister killed was even lower. I started to cry, as I stood up and started to open the portal, "YOU WANT IT OPEN!?", I yelled, as I pressed the button. The force was strong, and it was sucking the safety glass. It eventually shattered and everyone was grabbing something so they didn't get sucked into the portal. The demon was just standing there, happy I opened the portal, but not realizing what I'd done yet. I was standing in front of the control panel, wind trying to pull me into the void. The demon came and lifted me up, "You thought you could trick me…? Well, I'll show you what happens to those who try to outsmart me.", he said, as he started to fly into the void with me in his hand. I struggled and tried to fight but nothing I did worked. I screamed, as I was enveloped in darkness.

BRAD: I couldn't believe what we had just witnessed. I wanted to scream Lori's name, but I remembered she caused all of this. I didn't want to say she got what she deserved, but with everything I'd experienced, I had to accept that this was ALL Lori's fault. Roxy's brother, Teric, was helping her stand. Roxy was looking at the big blue spiral that was down beneath us. It was a blackhole just a few seconds ago. A blackhole that Lori was flown into against her will, by a demon. A security team stormed into the room. We pointed our guns at them, and another man came running from behind them, "DROP YOUR GUNS!", he yelled, and the guards lowered their weapons. "I saw everything. They're both gone. For good. They can't hurt this world. You all, go home. Never talk about this. That's it.", said the man, running his hands through his hair. "Who are you?", I asked. "Husan Martin. Don't worry, I'll take care of everything.", he said, directing us to leave, as a clean up crew was also coming into the room. Roxy approached Husan, and I didn't hear what she said, but he nodded, and she nodded for us to leave.

CHAPTER 12

DEATH OF STEPHANIE AND LORI'S DISAPPEARANCE

BRAD: It was a weird two weeks. Mara and I had grown close. Of course we were already seeing each other, but once I told her about how I was from another Earth, where we had children and were married, she became the Mara I had always known. I was happy as could be. With all the sex Mara and I were having, we were bound to have our children all over again. I just hoped it was the same kids from before. I missed them. Roxy had started working at Next Level Advancements. Husan was the new CEO and gave her a very important task; Get rid of everything pertaining to the Bradys or Lori Segrin. She was on top of it. Chrys was working as her assistant, and dating Teric, Roxy's brother. Everything was settling down, and I couldn't believe how lucky I was. Teric, Chrys, and Roxy were like our family. We had a bond that I couldn't explain. Knowing Roxy had some of Lori in her, it was like Lori was still here with us, but Roxy wasn't Lori. Roxy was caring, and I had a feeling she was going to be great at NLA. Roxy was really happy I had Mara again. Also, as it turns out, Harold was also alive here on this Earth, but he wasn't the same exact Harold, even though he was carrying out the same type of work for Stephanie and Lori here. Kidnapping, torture, and murder. Roxy and Husan had him arrested. They are dealing with all the legal crap brought on by Stephanie and Lori. Speaking of Stephanie, Keith Ledgewin is believed to have murdered her, but with Lori and Keith being gone, the authorities believe they were working together. I sometimes thought about what Lori was going through. She was pulled into Hell, so was she in Hell? I tried not to think about it too much, because it did nothing but stress me out. Where do we go when we die? Tommy said we go to the Astral Plane, but that's where the gate to Hell is, right? Most of this was brought up when I was being questioned. After all, I was Lori's boyfriend. I had no answers, seeing as they wouldn't believe me anyway. I just told them the last time I saw Lori was at the hospital. The camera footage proves that. So, they had no more questions for me. But one day, someone different showed up. It was a private detective. I was quite surprised, but I invited them into the apartment. I went and sat at the table near the kitchen. Mara was at work. "So, can I just call you Brad?", "Sure, I have no problem. So, what questions did you have for me?", "You were dating Lori Segrin, so, what can you tell me about her?", "She's long gone. I haven't seen her. And I'm sure you know I'm in a different relationship.", "Yes, yes, of course. I understand that, Brad. But you see, it's been a month, and I was hired to find Keith Ledgewin. You see, he had a woman he was seeing who said he started acting strange one day, and he mentioned Lori's name several times. He seemed afraid of something, and that was the last time she saw him. The next time she heard anything about him, he was being accused of murdering Stephanie Brady. Now, help me fill in some gaps. You were at the hospital the same day. You were there to see Keith Ledgewin. I've already spoken with some people that day. Did you believe Lori was cheating on you?", "I was cheating on her.", I said, confused. I understood he was just trying to find Keith, but why would he think I'd know more than I'm saying? "Listen, something about the story doesn't make any sense. I'm just going to tell you; Lori has been found, but not Keith. Only Lori. And she is incapable of speech. She just mumbles incoherently and doesn't seem to know where she is. She has panic attacks, and refuses to see any doctor or anybody else. She has only been asking for you, Brad.", said the detective. "Me? Wait, what do you mean you found her?", "A naked woman was found about fifty-eight miles from here in someone's backyard. Cops were called. Turns out, the lady was none other than Lori Segrin. How she got there, nobody knows, she hasn't said. But she keeps saying your name, so I'm assuming that maybe bringing you can help me find Keith.". I didn't know what to think. This was all really sudden. "I have to make some calls, but I'll go.", I said. The first person I called was Roxy, "Roxy, Lori is back. But she is in a mental institution.", "I know. I was notified about her yesterday. I didn't want to burden you. How did you find out?", she asked. I told her about the detective. "Brad, I don't think you should go. There is no point.", "I have to see her.", "What about Mara?", "I'll tell her later.", I said, as I nodded that I was going to go with the detective.

As we were driving, I had to ask, "So, she has only been asking for me, and hasn't said anything at all about Keith?", "No. Why did you want to see him that day? Be honest with me, Brad. I don't think you're a bad guy, but you definitely know more than you're telling.", "I'll tell you once I speak with Lori.", I said, knowing that it was better to wait. As we pulled into the parking lot of the institution, I couldn't stop thinking once again about what Lori was going through. We got out of the car and headed inside. There was a nurse who recognized the detective, "This is Brad.", he said. "Oh, good. Maybe you can finally get her to say something.", said the nurse. We walked through the door that took you to the patient rooms. I was looking through some of the windows. Some patients were just doing random things in their rooms, but they all had straitjackets on. Finally, we came to Lori's and my jaw dropped. Her hair, which was usually always nicely done or even in a ponytail, was wild, and her face looked like sandpaper was applied to her face then ripped off. Her pretty features were still visible, but her skin had a sort of dead look, with some of the skin on her face peeling. As the door opened, I couldn't believe this was the same woman I was in a relationship with just two months ago. She looked up at me, "BRAD!", she yelled, now standing and falling at my feet, "Brad, you're here…", she said, crying. "Lori, what happened to you?", I asked, kneeling down and putting my hands on her arms. "Living souls don't belong in Hell, Brad. I was brought back… But he's here… No. I can't talk about him…", "What can you talk about? Who is here?", "The demon. I can't say his name. It's cursed… He'll come for me. I can't talk about him, and that's ALL THEY WANT!", yelled Lori, pointing at the detective and the nurse. "They just want to know where Keith is, Lori.", "He's dead. I killed him when the demon entered his body. Brad, you have to listen to me; He's going to take souls for Hell. It's my fault. I opened the portal, and now he's going to take souls. Brad, do you still love me?", asked Lori, looking up at me with hope in her eyes. "Lori, I'm with someone else…", I said. Lori immediately stood and tried to attack me. She tried to bite me, but I moved out of the way, and we all rushed out the room, as the nurse closed the door back. "BRAD…! YOU'RE ALL GOING TO

HELL! I'VE BEEN THERE! I'VE SEEN IT! YOU'RE ALL GOING!",
said Lori, who started to laugh maniacally.

Later that night, I told Mara about the experience, "You should have
listened to Roxy and not gone.", "But I believe Lori, Mara. The demon is
amongst us.", "And what do you plan to do? You said that the moment you
saw that thing, he just waved his hand and you all were powerless. You
can't do anything, Sweetie. Just move on.", said Mara, kissing my head,
then turning over to sleep. I did the same.

It was dark outside. Except for one street lamp post. It was lit, and under
it was a man wearing a tux and a fedora. He motioned for me to come near. As
I did, I felt dread. "Brad, good to see you.", said Keith. "What do you want?",
"I'm not here to hurt you. I'm not the demon. It's really me. But I'm here to give
you a message; Leave Lori alone. She got what she deserved, and is continuing
to get what she deserves. I'm happy where I'm at, but she is the reason, and
where I am, the boss doesn't take kindly to people taking lives from others.",
"Are you saying…?", "Just live, Brad. Not many people get chances like yours.
You should be dead on that other Earth, but instead, you're alive, and you
get to have your children all over again, and you get to see them grow this
time. Because without Lori and Stephanie, the parallel Earths are safe now.
Lori messed with forces that were beyond Human comprehension. She sure
learned that the hard way. Good luck, Brad.", said Keith, now disappearing. I
woke up, and for a split second, couldn't move. I looked into the corner, and
saw a shadow. As soon as I freaked out, I was able to move and the shadow
was gone. Mara, my beautiful wife was next to me, and I saw on her dresser
stand, a pregnancy test. I laid down and breathed a sigh of relief.